Machines at Work
Fire Trucks

by Maria T. Schmidt

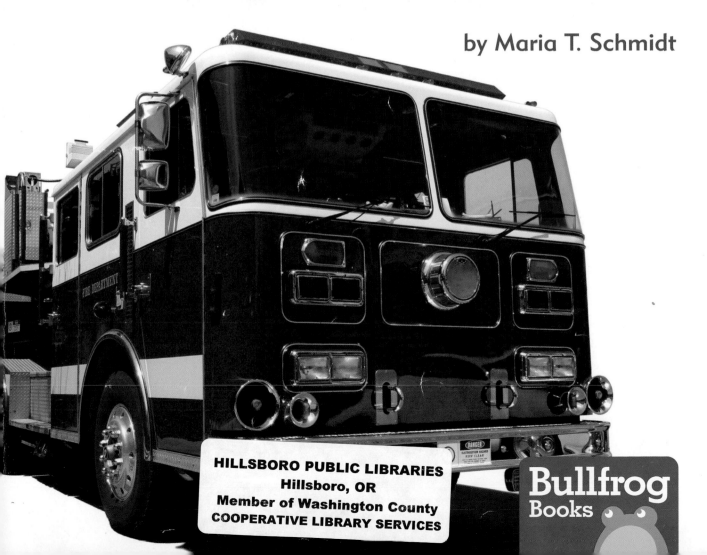

Bullfrog
Books

Ideas for Parents and Teachers

Bullfrog Books give children practice reading informational text at the earliest levels. Repetition, familiar words, and photo labels support early readers.

Before Reading

- Discuss the cover photo. What does it tell them?

- Look at the picture glossary together. Read and discuss the words.

Read the Book

- "Walk" through the book and look at the photos. Let the child ask questions.

- Read the book to the child, or have him or her read independently.

After Reading

- Prompt the child to think more. Ask: Have you ever seen a fire truck drive by? What did it look like? What did it sound like?

Bullfrog Books are published by Jump!
5357 Penn Avenue South
Minneapolis, MN 55419
www.jumplibrary.com

Library of Congress Cataloging-in-Publication Data
Schmidt, Maria T.
 Fire trucks / by Maria T. Schmidt.
   p. cm. — (Bullfrog books. Machines at work)
 Audience: K to grade 3
 Summary: "This photo-illustrated book for early readers describes different types of fire trucks and how they are each suited for fighting fires in different areas. Includes picture glossary"— Provided by publisher. 5548 4322
 Includes bibliographical references and index.
 ISBN 978-1-62031-020-5 (hardcover : alk. paper)
 1. Fire engines—Juvenile literature. I. Title.
 TH9372.S36 2013
 628.9'259--dc23   2012008574

Series Editor: Rebecca Glaser
Series Designer: Ellen Huber
Photo Researcher: Heather Dreisbach

Photo Credits
Alamy, 11, 23br; Dreamstime, 6–7; Getty Images, cover, 4, 13; iStockphoto, 22, 23bl; Science Photo Library, 18, 23ml; Shutterstock, 1, 3, 5, 8, 9, 12, 15, 16, 17, 20, 23tl, 23tr, 23mr, 24; Superstock, 21

Printed in the United States of America at Corporate Graphics, North Mankato, Minnesota.
7-2012 • PO 1122
10 9 8 7 6 5 4 3 2 1

Table of Contents

A Trip to the Fire Station

Jan's class is on a trip.

They are at a fire station.

They learn about fire trucks.

Each truck has a job.

Amy sees a pumper truck.

It pumps water from a fire hydrant.

Tanker trucks do not need hydrants.

They carry water to a fire.

tank

A ladder truck is tall.

The tallest reaches ten stories!

An air tanker
goes higher.

It fills its tank
as it flies.

It skims water
from a lake.

Fireboats pump
water from the sea.

They spray out
fast and hard.

Sam likes the brush truck.

It drives on rough ground.

It fights wildfires.

Firefighters need fire trucks.

They help save lives.

Parts of a Fire Truck

ladder
A structure used for climbing to reach high places.

hose
A long bendy tube that water goes through.

locker
A cabinet in a truck that holds tools.

water pump
A machine that sucks and pushes water along hoses.

cab
The part of a truck where a driver sits.

Picture Glossary

air tanker
An airplane that can scoop up water to fight fires from the sky.

ladder truck
A fire truck with a very tall ladder.

brush truck
A small fire truck used to fight wildfires that is easy to drive in tight spots.

pumper truck
A fire truck that pumps water from a fire hydrant.

fireboat
A boat built to fight fires.

tanker truck
A fire truck that has a large water tank.

Index

To Learn More

Learning more is as easy as 1, 2, 3.

1) Go to www.factsurfer.com

2) Enter "fire truck" into the search box.

3) Click the "Surf" button to see a list of websites.

With factsurfer.com, finding more information is just a click away.